DISNEY Sofia the First

Living in a Royal World

13 14 15 EAS 39016 10 9 8 7 6 5 4 3 2 1

Welcome to the family, Sofia!

Princess Amber and Prince James are twins.

All hail Princess Sofia!

Which picture of Sofia is different?

A

B

C

D

5 **Dalmatian Press**

Answer: B

© Disney

King Roland says there will be a ball in Sofia's honor.

The king gives Sofia the Amulet of Avalor.
She promises to always wear it!

Cedric, The Royal Sorcerer

Cedric wants Sofia's magic amulet.

"The amulet is so pretty, Sofia. May I hold it?"
asks Cedric.

The Magic Amulet

Find the best words to complete the rhyme.

For each deed performed, for better or

_____.

Which word comes next?

Word   Work   Worse

A power is granted, a blessing or

_____.

Which word comes next?

Care   Curse   Call

Dalmatian Press

Answers: Worse, Curse

"Oh, Merlin's mushrooms!" says Cedric.

12

Will Sofia be ready for the ball?
She doesn't know how to dance.

James tries to teach Sofia to dance.

Complete the number pattern in the dance steps.

A 1 2 1 2 1

B 3 3 4 4 3

C 5 6 7 8 6

Sofia asks Cedric for a dancing spell.

16

Cedric wants to trick Sofia and take the amulet.

Sofia hopes the spell works!

Draw what Cedric is thinking about.

When Cedric's spell backfires, Sofia gets
a quick dance lesson from Amber!

Princess Sofia

Sofia dances with the king.

Decode the message by matching the letters to the numbers.

Sof___ ___ d___nc___d
     3   1   1   2

l___k___ ___ ___ r___ ___l
  3   2   1   2   1

pr___nc___ss!
   3   2

1=a 2=e 3=i

Answer: Sofia danced like a real princess!

Princess Sofia wakes up.

Time to get dressed.

Help Sofia find her way to the dining hall.

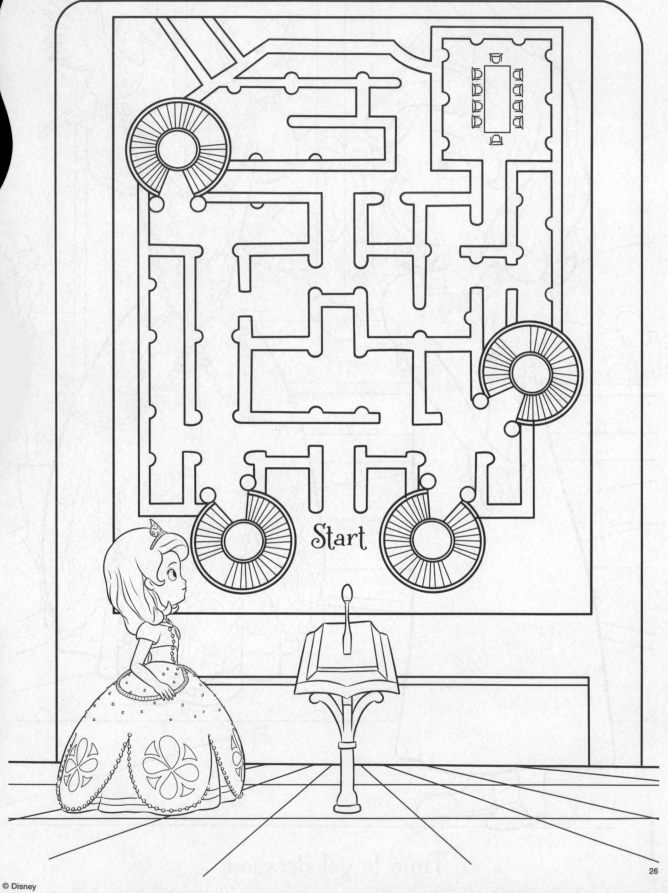

Start

Baileywick takes Sofia to breakfast.

So many choices!

Time for school.

The Royal Coach

Connect the dots to complete the flying horse.

...lcome to Royal Prep—the Royal Preparatory Academy

Headmistresses Flora, Fauna, and Merryweather

Amber's best friends—Clio and Hildegard

Unscramble the names!

O F A S I

_ _ _ _ _

Ǝ M R B A

_ _ _ _ _

O L I C

_ _ _ _

M Ǝ S A J

_ _ _ _ _

Answers: Sofia, Amber, Clio, James

Hurry to class.

Every princess must know how to curtsy.

Arts & Crafts

Draw what Sofia is painting.

Sofia makes new friends at Royal Prep.

Professor Popov's Dance Class

Recess!

Put the pictures in order by numbering them 1-4.

A

_____

B

_____

C

_____

D

_____

Answers: 1-B, 2-A, 3-D, 4-C

Amber and Clio share a secret.

Hildegard gets an "A" in Fan Fluttering.

Time to Study

Find and circle 4 pictures of Sofia and 3 books.

Be careful, Sofia!

Magic Class

Learning to be a princess is not easy!

Home Sweet Home

Sofia and Clover

Robin and Mia

Find and circle 7 items that begin with the letter B.

A Royal Tea Party

Oops!

Amber wonders if Sofia will ever be a real princess.

Match the shadows to their owners.

1

2

3

A

B

C

Answers: 1-C, 2-A, 3-B

© Disney

Baileywick announces that dinner is served.

Sofia has so much to learn!

Count the tableware.

How many forks do you see? ☐

How many knives do you see? ☐

How many spoons do you see? ☐

Add all the silverware together. ☐

Dalmatian Press

Answers: 6 forks, 3 knives, 3 spoons; Total = 12

"How was your day, dear?"

Sofia misses her village friends.

Ruby and Jade

A Royal Sleepover

There are 6 differences between the two pictures. Can you find them?

66

Answers: 1-Clover, 2- cake instead of tea in Sofia's hand, 3- teapot, 4- table legs, 5- saucer missing, 6- curler missing

A Magical Puppet Show

A Royal Makeover

Best Friends Forever!

Homework with Vivian—Build a Dream Castle

Draw your own Dream Castle.

Look down and across to find the words listed below.

```
M O M S O F I A R
I J B R O B I N O
R A M B E R N C L
A M G B K U G C A
N E O U F B P L N
D S E P J Y Q O D
A T Y N A D Z V E
H W A I D J U E Y
H I L D E G A R D
```

Amber   Roland

Clover   Jade

Hildegard   Ruby

Miranda   James

Robin   Sofia

Crackle!

New Friends

Crackle's Special Talent

Find and circle 5 pictures of Crackle and 3 pictures of corn.

The Tri-Kingdom Picnic

Princess Jun and Prince Jin from Wei-Ling

Prince Khalid and Princess Maya from Khaldoun.

The Prince and Princesses of Enchancia!